My Fi[rst]

Match

CHRISTOPHER
ABBOTT

I was unbelievably excited, a smile beaming on my face. My dad had told me all about it, his and grandad's favourite place.

I had my tea and got wrapped up, a hat to warm my ears.

"Don't let him out your sight", shrieked mum. I thought I saw some tears.

It was getting dark outside, it should be time for bed. Would it be loud? Would it be fun? Thoughts whizzing round my head.

We set off on our merry way, something gave me quite a scare. People walking on the road, they didn't seem to care!

I'd never seen this many folk, how big must this stadium be? It reminded me of a marching army that I'd seen on TV.

As tall as Everest, as bright as
fire, they're really quite a sight.
Dad says they're called floodlights
and illuminate the pitch at night.

We were getting closer now, I could feel the tension growing. I gripped dad's hand as tight as I could, I think the nerves were showing.

The noise inside was deafening, I'd never heard my old man sing.

The greatest thing
I'd ever seen, the
beginning of my
football story.

I stood on my seat and clapped my heroes, they were only over there. I couldn't take my eyes off them, I couldn't help but stare.

The chance of sleep? No chance at all. Ref, what did you do?
We missed a pen, we hit the post, how did we draw 2-2?

For Rory and Amelia

First published in the United Kingdom in 2021 by
The Choir Press

ISBN 978-1-78963-261-3

CPSIA information can be obtained
at www.ICGtesting.com
Printed in the USA
LVHW070617031121
702254LV00005B/6